HURON COUNTY LIBRARY

W9-CHI-303

Date Due

JUL 23 1998	SEP 19 '00	
OCT 23 1998	FEB 1 4 2004	
MAY 2 '00		

BRODART   Cat. No. 23 233   Printed in U.S.A.

DISCARD

JP
Butle

2086

Butler, Geoff, 1945-
   The hangashore / Geoff Butler. --Toronto : Tundra
Books, c1998.
   1 v. (unpaged) : col. ill.

905783   ISBN:0887764444

1. Down syndrome - Juvenile fiction. 2. Fishing -
Juvenile fiction. 3. Newfoundland - Juvenile fiction.
I. Title

65   98JUN12   3559/cl   1-523386

HURON COUNTY LIBRARY

DISCARD

THE HANGASHORE

Geoff Butler

TUNDRA BOOKS

JUN 2 2 '98

Copyright © 1998 by Geoff Butler

Published in Canada by Tundra Books, *McClelland & Stewart Young Readers*, 481 University Avenue, Toronto, Ontario M5G 2E9

Published in the United States by Tundra Books of Northern New York, P.O. Box 1030, Plattsburgh, New York 12901

Library of Congress Catalog Number: 97-62179

All rights reserved. The use of any part of this publication reproduced, transmitted in any form or by any means, electronic, mechanical, photocopying, recording, or otherwise, or stored in a retrieval system, without the prior written consent of the publisher – or, in case of photocopying or other reprographic copying, a licence from the Canadian Copyright Licensing Agency – is an infringement of the copyright law.

Canadian Cataloguing in Publication Data

Butler, Geoff, 1945-
   The hangashore

ISBN 0-88776-444-4

I. Title.

PS8553.U699H36 1998   jC813'.54   C97-932438-6
PZ7.B87Ha 1998

We acknowledge the support of the Canada Council for the Arts for our publishing program.

We acknowledge the financial support of the Government of Canada through the Book Publishing Industry Development Program for our publishing activities.

Design by Sari Ginsberg

Printed in Hong Kong by South China Printing Co. Ltd.

1 2 3 4 5 6   03 02 01 00 99 98

This book is dedicated to my Uncle Fred Earle of Lewisporte, Newfoundland, who has spent much of his life enjoying and documenting Newfoundland culture.

Thanks to Chick Caldwell, Nat Tileston and Wayne Boucher for being my models for the illustrations; to Philip Woods for permitting me to use his photograph of a whale as a reference; to May Cutler for encouraging me to write stories of Newfoundland; to Kathy Lowinger for her perceptive editorial suggestions; and to Sue Tate for her helpful copyediting.

Acknowledgment is also given to Newfoundland writer, Ted Russell (1904-1977). In his play, *The Hangashore*, he describes a hangashore as someone who's "too bad to be called a good-for-nothin' and not bad enough to be called a sleeveen."

In the *Dictionary of Newfoundland English*, a hangashore is defined as "an unlucky person deserving pity," or a worthless fellow who's too lazy to fish, or someone who's idle and mischievous. A person who is deceitful, mean, and more of a rascal is called a sleeveen.

The church towered above everything else on the island. Its steeple stood steadfast above the horizon, and fishermen used it as a beacon to guide them home, just as they strained to hear its bell if they were lost in fog or caught in a storm. Besides beckoning the parishioners to Sunday worship, the bell alerted the islanders to emergencies. Soon it would alert them to the end of the Second World War.

In 1945 the war was always on everyone's mind. Whenever the coastal boat arrived with mail, cargo, and passengers, the islanders would gather on the wharf to catch up on the latest news.

One such morning, a special passenger stood on the deck of the coastal steamer. It was the new magistrate from England who came to take up his posting on this small Newfoundland island. As he looked down at the people assembled on the wharf, he thought, 'Hmm, they must have had prior notice of my arrival. It is encouraging to get such a welcome, and to see such community interest in the administration of justice.' Then he thought further, 'Of course, it's not surprising, considering that so many who live here still refer to England as the mother country.'

Magistrate Mercer had brought not only an educated mind to dispense justice, but also the feeling that he had to refine the behavior of the colonials. He was therefore conscious of setting a good example.

That Sunday, when he walked up the church aisle, he did so with slow, measured steps, and took an elaborate bow to the altar before stepping into his pew.

"Mind the magistrate," parents told their children, "and you'll learn how to act proper."

The front pew on the right was the magistrate's. The one on the left was for the minister's family. A parishioner had once complimented the minister, Reverend Payne, on how his whole family was involved in the church services. "You got all hands busy – you deliverin' from the pulpit, yer missus pounding on the organ, and yer young ones up there in the singing seats. Then you got John in his pew, welcomin' all aboard."

John was always cheerful and talkative, but he giggled a bit too much and his speech was not clear. He was sixteen. People said he was slow or not right in the head, but all agreed that he was of a good nature.

While one could never be quite sure what John would say next, Magistrate Mercer chose his words carefully. His responses in church were given so slowly and loudly, they fell behind the fast dialect of the islanders. He was not to be hurried, and everyone learned to wait. They'd whisper, "His Lordship's in fine trim this morning" or, "No one's going to rush he, that's for certain."

Magistrate Mercer became even more self-absorbed when the prayer asking God's blessings for "all who are set in authority over us" was said. This solemn moment was once disrupted by John who whispered loudly, "Psst, Yer Majesty. That's you we're praying for." The magistrate raised his head slightly and said nothing.

During one afternoon service, the magistrate was speaking oh so slowly during a prayer, even John got exasperated. "You're as slow as cold molasses today," he said. "If you don't hurry up, it'll be dark before we get out of here."

Magistrate Mercer glared and, from that day on, took a particular dislike to him.

The next day, the magistrate was in court. A layabout named Mose was brought before him on a charge of hunting rabbits out of season. "The constable found you trying to sell a brace of skinned rabbits to people disembarking from the coastal steamer," thundered the magistrate. "What do you have to say for yourself?"

"May God strike me dead if I'm lyin'," retorted Mose. "The constable's got a pretty sharp eye, but perhaps his hearing's not so good. You see, Yer Honor, I was only chargin' for the price of skinnin' them."

"And I suppose you'll mock this court by saying you just pulled these rabbits out of a black hat. Well, maybe you can pull some hard cash from that magic cap of yours for the fine I'm going to levy."

"Well, now, Yer Honor, that's a bit more than I'm up to, seein' as my pockets ain't seen naught but coppers in a dog's age." Then Mose thought for awhile and added, "But I'd be pleased to settle accounts with you in other ways. Perhaps I could take Yer Honor on his rounds about the coast for a spell, with my boat, till I pays off my debt."

The magistrate eyed him carefully. "Done!" he pronounced, for he had not been looking forward to traveling his circuit alone, at least not until he'd gotten better accustomed to the area.

Meanwhile, Reverend Payne tried to console John who felt rejected by the icy stare the magistrate had given him. "Perhaps you shouldn't go bothering the magistrate for awhile. He's a busy man, with no time for trifles. Besides, not having children of his own, he's not used to being spoken to the way you did."

Others in the community were not so forgiving. "There's a slippery stone at his door, for sure," they said.

What really set them off was the day the Church Lads' Brigade marched to church for a special V-E Day service. An iceberg floated by and Union Jacks snapped briskly in the wind. Inside, the church was packed, and the small contingent of boys paraded proudly up the aisle. They settled into the reserved front pews, and the color party stepped forward, trooping their flags to the strains of "God Save the King."

The magistrate, however, refused to give up his pew.

"The integrity of my office must be upheld," he maintained.

"But Magistrate Mercer," the warden said, "no one questions your authority. It's just a matter of having these local lads sit in the front pews for one service. Makes them feel special, you know. It won't be long until the soldiers return from overseas, and we'll be wanting to honor them with a special service too. Please don't say you won't give up your pew for them."

"Wars come and go," the magistrate replied. "Of course we're all grateful to the soldiers fighting them, but institutions are the bedrock of society. Like, I dare say, your rock of an island."

"The only rock he's likely to be," someone said angrily, "is more like a sunker."

Because John had given up his pew to the Church Lads' Brigade, the magistrate felt this added to the tarnish on his character in the eyes of the islanders. His dislike for John increased.

Reverend Payne decided he'd better talk to John about it. "Sometimes," he said, "a person can be as smart as a bee, but that doesn't mean he's better than anyone else. Take Magistrate Mercer, for instance. You might wish you had his head, but he could learn a thing or two from you, John."

"From me, Father? Now wouldn't that be a laugh and a half. You're putting me on, aren't you? His head's full of learning."

"Now, look. You can go anywhere and be as welcome as the flowers in May."

"Well, the magistrate goes everywhere, doesn't he?"

"That he does, John, as part of his job. And people respect him for that. But I'm talking about what he's like as a person. Now, promise me you won't ever repeat this, but Magistrate Mercer is as cold as a dog's nose."

"I don't think he likes me, Father."

"Maybe he doesn't like himself, John. You've shown him what he's not. Just like wars show us a part of ourselves that we don't like. You know, young boys brought up here on our island, just happy to be going fishing and, before you know it, they're off somewhere fighting people they don't even know. The sad part is that those on one side forget that the ordinary people on the other side are just like them. See, John, one thing the magistrate can learn from you is how to get along with people. Enough talk for now. The war's over and the soldiers will be coming home. It's time for a celebration."

When the soldiers arrived, the magistrate was among the official party that stood at the wharf to greet them as they walked down the gangplank of the coastal steamer. He wore his courtroom robes and read a proclamation of thanks for their answering the call to service, for their sacrifices, and for their courage.

But that Sunday, when the special service honoring the returning soldiers was held, the magistrate again sat in his front pew. "Stay the course," he kept reminding himself. "These people respect a person with determination."

The soldiers sat in the rows behind him but, on the left-hand side of the aisle, they also sat in the front pew. Though it was clear that the congregation disapproved of the magistrate's refusal to give up *his* pew, nothing was said. The emotion of the moment overshadowed such petty affairs. The war was over. Nothing else mattered.

But John was clearly upset at what he perceived as ingratitude on the magistrate's part.

He strode over, bold as brass, to the magistrate's pew and spoke so all could hear. "You look lonely as a gull on a rock up here in yer pew, all by yerself, Majesty Mercy. Why not shove over now, and I'll keep you company, seein' as how's I gave up my own pew for our soldiers. But I have to say, it'll take all the religion that's in me to sit down by a hangashore."

The magistrate was clearly taken aback. Hearing snickers behind him, he reluctantly moved over, his face as red as a beet. But he was not the center of attention that day. Nothing short of the roof caving in could have detracted from the joyousness of the service. Tears flowed and the singing soared in heartfelt thanks for the end of the war and the return of loved ones to this small coastal community.

The magistrate was still fuming as he left the church. Coming up to the Reverend who was shaking hands with the departing parishioners, he ignored the minister's outstretched hand. "That boy should be in an institution, perhaps at the Mental Hospital up in St. John's. I intend to see about it on my next trip. It's too bad when a God-fearing person can't go to church without being harassed by some half-wit. Good morning, sir."

Standing nearby on the steps outside, John couldn't help but hear. Be taken from his home? Sent away from the island? Choking back tears, he ran home as fast as he could, muttering, "No one's takin' me to any institution." He stocked some provisions in a brin bag and ran down toward the wharf.

Then he spied Mose, who was at the wharf getting his boat ready to pay his debt. The next morning he was supposed to ferry the magistrate about.

"Oh, good mornin', Johnnie lad," said Mose. "Yer in a mighty hurry, but yer not as fast as the word that's travelin' about ya. I heard you did a brave thing in church this mornin', moving the magistrate off his high throne. No doubt he's sayin' to himself that yer a real Payne, eh? In the neck, that is. But a lotta people, I dare say, wish they'd had the gumption to be in yer shoes." Mose continued, "Now where might ye be off to, lad?"

"Oh, Mose, you got to promise not to tell, 'cept you can tell Mother and Father I'm safe. His Majesty wants to send me away, but I'm not going to let him, not me. I'm taking Father's boat over to Li'l Cove before he gets around to it. I'll stay in one of the fishermen's shacks there for a spell."

"Now listen here, me son," cautioned Mose. "Don't you go doing anything foolish. No one's goin' to be takin' you away against yer will."

"I wasn't scared of him in church today, but I'm scared of him now, Mose. I s'pose I mocked him in front of people. He's a powerful man. His word carries a lot of weight."

"Well, so do the Reverend's, sure."

"But they'll say he's kin and 'twon't matter. I'm goin', Mose, for a few days anyway."

John jumped into the tender and rowed out to the motorboat. He didn't look back as he started up the engine and headed toward Little Cove.

Early the next day, the magistrate was on his way to the mainland. His job required much traveling, as did that of the Reverend – over land by foot, across tickles and bays by boat or, in wintertime, on the ice by horse and sleigh.

Mose had secretly liked this trip to the mainland, for there he could stock up on spirits. Not that he couldn't wet his whistle at home with his homebrew but, if his friends had gotten their "package" from the Board of Liquor Control, he'd have the "proper stuff" to drink.

After tying up at the government wharf, the magistrate said, "Be ready to leave tomorrow at noon, Mose."

"I be at your beck and call, Yer Honor. Always ready and waitin', that's me."

"Good man," said the magistrate, not sounding convinced.

As the magistrate walked out of sight, Mose wasted no time in looking for booze. The next day, he was "well under the influence" and couldn't hide it. "Have you been drinking, man?" Magistrate Mercer asked as he got into the boat.

"Don't mind me, Yer Honor," replied Mose, "I just had a nip or two. Now, don't ye go worryin'. I knows these waters like the palm of my hand."

The magistrate was clearly displeased, and not much more was spoken between them. Perhaps to ease the tension, he started whistling a tune.

"Fer heaven's sake, Yer Honor," cried Mose, "don't go whistling on the water. 'Tis bad luck'll befall us, fer sure."

But the magistrate paid him no mind until they were approaching a favorite fishing ground of the islanders, not far off Little Cove. Mose said, "Would Yer Honor like some fresh cod fer his supper? Perhaps jig one himself?"

"By the looks of you, I'll have to do it. You don't appear fit to do much of anything."

"Well, I can throw the grapnel overboard, and while yer jiggin' there, I'll just catch meself a few winks."

Not far away, John had been jigging for cod himself, while mulling over what the magistrate had said about him. "I s'pose if His Majesty says so, I must be as foolish as a caplin, and stunned to boot. I am not worth anything to anybody."

Suddenly he heard a commotion. He looked about and saw a boat moving quickly through the water, its bow down low. Immediately he guessed what the problem was and sped toward it.

Meanwhile, Mose was yelling, "Yer Honor, I bet this is the biggest catch ye ever got. A whale, I'd say, caught up in the grapnel rope. If he don't untangle hisself soon, he's sure to pull we under, and if I don't manage to cut the rope soon, that's exactly what's goin' to happen."

In the state he was in from drinking, coupled with the unpredictable rocking back and forth of the boat, Mose tried to keep his balance. Grabbing his knife, he crawled toward the bow. As salt spray stung his eyes and waves pounded over him, a sudden lurch of the boat sent him over the side into the water. The boat and the magistrate sped past him.

"Say a prayer, Yer Honor," shouted Mose, as he thrashed about in the water. "One fer ye and one fer me."

By this time, John had arrived. He circled round Mose, threw him a rope and hauled him in.

"Better get to the magistrate fast, John me son, or he'll be another Jonah."

Then to himself he mumbled, "I told he not to whistle on the water."

"C'mon here, Mose, and take over," yelled John. "Try to catch up to him before he goes under. If you can get alongside, I'll lean over and cut the rope."

Quickly they closed the gap between the two boats. 'Poor blighter,' thought Mose, as he saw the fear in the magistrate's face. 'He don't have the sense to jump overboard. Perhaps he'd rather be in the whale's company than with we.'

The urgency of the situation had cleared Mose's mind from the effects of his drinking. Looking at the bow so low in the water, he smiled. "Hey, John b'y," he shouted, nodding toward the magistrate high in the stern. "He ain't so eager to sit in the front pew now."

Mose managed to bring the boat alongside. John quickly slashed the grapnel rope. Its end snapped and whipped through the air before settling into the turbulent wash of the whale. The magistrate's boat slowed to a stop.

Mose cut back the engine as John threw a line to the magistrate. After catching their breath, Mose said, "Ye were right Johnny-on-the-spot, John. We owes you a pile of thanks." Then he jumped into his own boat and began bailing out pails of water. He called to John, "Will ye be followin' us in?"

"I'll be in shortly, after I go get my things. You go on ahead."

On the way back, the magistrate was subdued. After awhile he said to Mose, "In church, he called me a hangashore. What's a hangashore, Mose?"

"Oh . . . it's just a . . . er . . . it depends on how it's used, sir."

"Well, it certainly didn't sound like any kind of a compliment. Go on, tell me."

"Beggin' yer pardon, Yer Honor, 'tis a pitiful person. And I should know, cause that's what I be. But ye be a better hangashore than me. No, I means, yer not as good a hangashore as me. Oh, ye knows what I means to say, sir. He was just put out with ye, sir, and said the first thing that popped into his head, 'cause I dare say he's been called a poor little hangashore himself more than once. But someone as stalwart in the community as ye wouldn't be a real hangashore. Now, me, I'm worthless and too lazy to fish, so I'm a proper hangashore."

The magistrate interjected, "He thinks I should be pitied?"

"Well, Yer Honor, John thought it something awful ye couldn't see fit to give up yer pew, cause he was so happy to let the soldiers sit in his, seein' it was their day."

Never having spoken to the magistrate before like this, Mose thought he'd get as much in as he could while the going was good. "Yer chains of office," he went on, "are so we can respect Yer Honor, not to bind ye up so that ye can't move aft or forward. The pity in it, sir, is he's got so little in his head and ye got so much, but he lets go and ye holds back. Why, sure, he's so happy just bein' alive, he thinks he's got a lot to be thankful fer and thinks nothing of showing it."

That evening, the magistrate walked up to the church. Slowly, as if not sure in his own mind what he was about, he lifted the door latch. He sat alone in his pew for a long time, then picked up the hymnbook. It opened to the hymn,

"All things bright and beautiful,

All creatures great and small,

All things wise and wonderful . . ."

Almost before he knew it, the magistrate made up his own words to finish the verse. Then, there in the empty church, he imagined John sitting in the pew across the aisle, and Magistrate Mercer found himself leaning over and whispering, "Psst, John." An instant later, he was singing, "And hangashores short and tall."

He smiled to himself, then decided to go over to the rectory to see John.

"Good evening, Reverend," said the magistrate. "I'd like to say I talked with the doctor about your young John. He said the walls of the Mental Hospital are as thick as fog in the outports and it would not be proper for a young man like John to be in such an institution, for there'd be no sun or winds to disperse the fog as there is around here."

Then Magistrate Mercer asked if he could have a few words with John.

When John came to the door, the magistrate shook his hand and said, "I want to thank you, John, for two things. One is for rescuing Mose and me. And the second thing, well, . . . it's a sort of rescue also. I know you'll understand when you see me sitting in the back pew this Sunday. And after that, if you wish, you can sit with me in my front pew anytime you feel like it."

0